Y0-AST-132

DISCARD

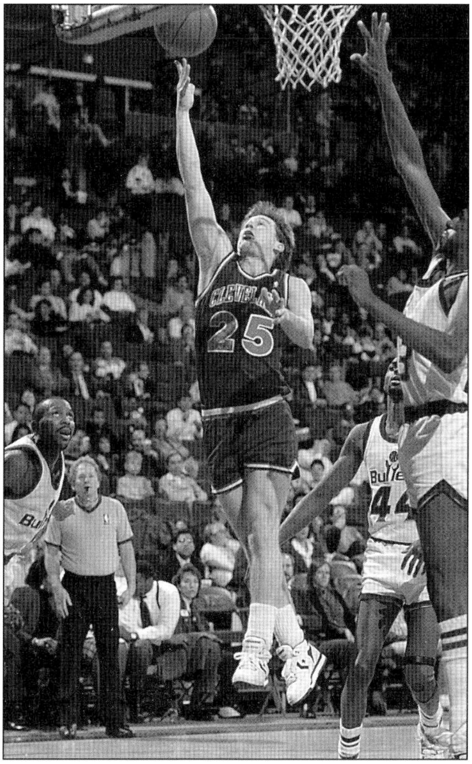

25
44

Cleveland Cavaliers

Richard Rambeck

CREATIVE EDUCATION

Published by Creative Education
123 South Broad Street, Mankato, Minnesota 56001
Creative Education is an imprint of The Creative Company

Designed by Rita Marshall

Photos by: Allsport Photography, Associated Press/Wide World Photos, NBA Photos, UPI/Corbis Bettmann, and SportsChrome.

Photo page 1: Mark Price
Photo title page: Vitaly Potapenko

Copyright © 1998 Creative Education.
International copyrights reserved in all countries.
No part of this book may be reproduced in any form without written permission from the publisher.
Printed in the United States of America.

Library of Congress Cataloging-in-Publication Data

Rambeck, Richard.
Cleveland Cavaliers / Richard Rambeck.
p. cm. — (NBA today)
Summary: Describes the background and history of the Cleveland Cavaliers pro basketball team to 1997.
ISBN 0-88682-870-8

1. Cleveland Cavaliers (Basketball team)—History—Juvenile literature.
[1. Cleveland Cavaliers (Basketball team)—History. 2. Basketball—History.]
I. Title. II. Series: NBA today (Mankato, Minn.)

GV885.52.C57R36 1997   96-53022
796.323'64'0977132—dc21

First edition

5 4 3 2 1

Cleveland is the largest city in Ohio, thanks in part to John D. Rockefeller. The wealthy industrialist founded Standard Oil near the mouth of Cleveland's Cuyahoga River in 1870. The presence of Standard Oil helped the city become a major port and a center of commerce. Located on the shores of Lake Erie, Cleveland is a docking point for ships carrying goods up the St. Lawrence Seaway.

In the 1950s, Cleveland had a population of nearly one million people and was the seventh-largest city in the United States. During the 1970s, however, Cleveland's population

Defensive stalwart Larry Nance.

Walt Wesley's 50-point performance against Cincinnati remains an all-time Cavalier high.

dropped. Hard economic times caused the city to become run-down, and many residents moved to more prosperous areas. Some comedians even began sarcastically referring to Cleveland as "the mistake by the lake."

Local leaders vowed to spruce up their town to lure businesses and people back to Cleveland. As a result, the city has been largely rebuilt. Cleveland has added parks, planted trees, and has torn down and rebuilt skyscrapers. The jokes that used to be told about Cleveland have been replaced with compliments, and the city is now the home of such attractions as the Rock and Roll Hall of Fame.

One of the aspects of Cleveland that people once kidded about was its National Basketball Association (NBA) franchise. During the early 1980s, the Cleveland Cavaliers were probably the worst team in pro basketball. The Cavaliers, or Cavs for short, were best known for trading their stars and receiving little in return. One year the NBA felt so sorry for the Cavaliers, it gave the team an extra first-round pick. Then, in the mid-1980s, brothers George and Gordon Gund bought the club from its former owner, the unpredictable Ted Stepien. Suddenly Cleveland's luck changed. The Cavaliers used the NBA draft to build an outstanding young team, led by Terrell Brandon and coach Mike Fratello. As the 1990s began, the once-awful Cavaliers were rebuilt into an exciting team with a bright future.

BRINGING THE NBA TO CLEVELAND

The Cavs were born on February 7, 1970, when a group of investors paid 3.7 million dollars for the right to install

Guard Bingo Smith.

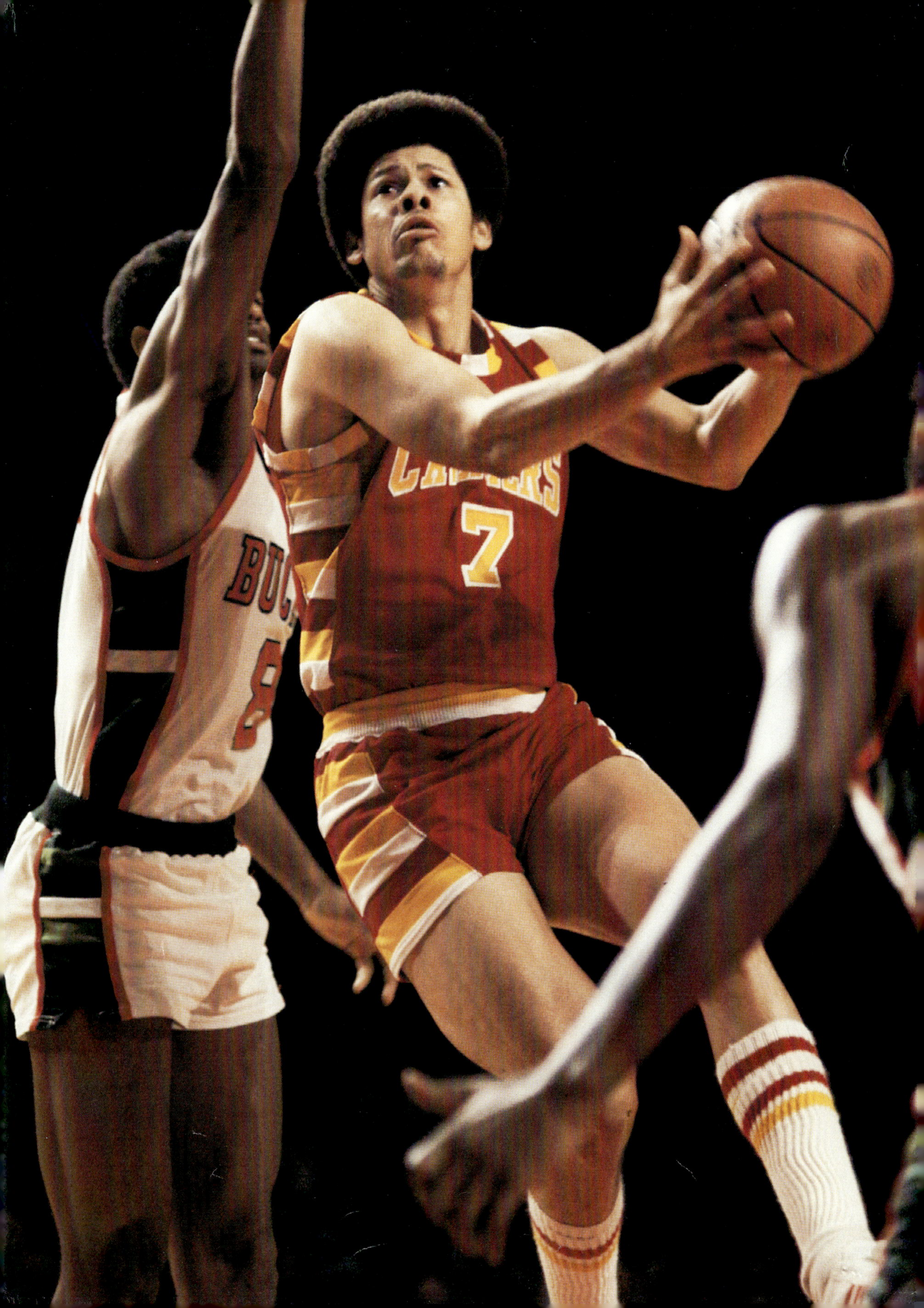

Rookie John Johnson represented the Cavs in the NBA All-Star Game.

the Cleveland Cavaliers as the seventeenth team in the NBA. The head of the group, Cleveland businessman Nicholas Mileti, knew it wouldn't be easy to make the city's sports fans notice the Cavs. Cleveland was known as a baseball and football town. Its baseball team, the Indians, had been playing in the American League since 1901, and its football franchise, the Browns, had been one of the best teams in the National Football League for more than 20 years.

Mileti worried that the Cavs wouldn't be able to "measure up to the Browns and Indians." Bill Fitch, who was hired as the team's first coach, told Mileti and the fans to be patient. "Winners aren't built overnight. Just remember," he joked, "my name is Fitch, not Houdini."

Fitch proved to be correct. There was no magic for the Cavs in their first few seasons in the NBA. In the early years of the franchise, Fitch tried to build the club around the talents of players picked in the expansion draft—players from the bottom of the rosters of other NBA teams. They included veteran center Walt Wesley and guards Bobby "Bingo" Smith and Butch Beard. The hodgepodge team lost the first 15 games of the 1970–71 season. The club's first victory finally came against Portland, another expansion team. Cleveland finished its first season with a 15–67 record.

PUTTING CARR IN THE DRIVER'S SEAT

After that terrible first year, the Cavs selected Notre Dame forward Austin Carr in the NBA draft. He proved to be an excellent choice. Carr was a scoring machine who had averaged 34.5 points a game during his college career.

Carr moved right into Cleveland's starting lineup. As a rookie, he didn't score as many points as he had in college, but he did average more than 20 a game. "Austin has certainly made my job easier," Fitch pointed out. "The man can flat-out fill the hoop." Unfortunately, Carr missed more than half the season with a broken foot. But despite his injury and absence from the court, he still made enough of an impression to be named to the NBA All-Rookie team.

With Carr and some other talented youngsters on the club, Fitch believed he had the makings of a pretty good team. What was missing, however, was an experienced leader on the court. So Fitch traded Butch Beard to the Seattle SuperSonics for veteran guard Lenny Wilkens. Wilkens had helped make the Sonics a winning team as both a player and a coach. "I think with some of the younger guys we can surprise a lot of people this year," Wilkens said of his new team. "This isn't an expansion team anymore—at least it doesn't have to be."

The Cavs posted a 32–50 record in 1972–73, winning nine more games than the year before. Little by little the city was starting to take to the young club, and attendance at Cavs games was on the rise. The Cavaliers needed to build fan support because the team was scheduled to move into a new arena in time for the 1974–75 season. Located in Richfield, a suburb of Cleveland, the Coliseum had almost 20,000 seats that club officials hoped to fill for each game. Before the move, however, the Cavs played one final season in ancient Cleveland Arena. (It was also Lenny Wilkens's last year as a player. He retired after averaging 16.4 points a game in 1973–74 and later turned to coaching.)

Veteran guard Lenny Wilkens ranked second in the league in assists with an 8.4 average.

Austin Carr, Cleveland's first standout.

Danny Ferry, a Cleveland star of the 1990s.

CAVS RISE TO THE TOP OF THE DIVISION

In his second season with the team, Jim Chones led the Cavs with 563 field goals.

Without Wilkens, Bill Fitch planned to build the team around Austin Carr, backed by forwards Jim Brewer and Campy Russell, center Jim Chones, and guards Dick Snyder and Jim Cleamons. None of these players was a superstar, but a superstar wouldn't have fit into coach Fitch's system. Fitch believed in close teamwork in which each man played a major role in the team's overall performance. The Cavs' unity suffered, however, when Carr went down with a knee injury 16 games into the 1974–75 season. Even without Carr, Cleveland won 40 games and nearly made the playoffs.

The following season, the Cavs added future Hall of Fame center Nate Thurmond to an already solid cast, and Austin Carr returned healthy to the lineup. The Cavaliers took off. Led by Carr's scoring and Thurmond's strong inside play, they rose to the top of the Central Division. Thurmond, who was called "Dr. Defense" by Cleveland fans, proved to be the perfect addition to the team. He provided the rebounding and shot-blocking that were needed to make Fitch's defensive philosophy work. Thurmond didn't worry much about whether he scored; he only cared about stopping the other team's center. "I'll guarantee you, Nate still makes life miserable for me," said Kareem Abdul-Jabbar. Thurmond's defense helped the Cavs post a 49–33 record, which was good enough to win the Central Division title. For the first time ever, the team was in the playoffs.

Cleveland fans flocked to the Richfield Coliseum in record numbers, filling the building for all of Cleveland's playoff games. In the first round, the Cavs won an incredibly close seven-game series against the Washington Bullets. Cleveland then took on the powerful Boston Celtics. The two teams split the first four games of the series before the Celtics turned it on and won the final two games. The Cavaliers' season was over, but the future looked very bright.

That future, however, was clouded by injuries during the 1976–77 and 1977–78 seasons. Cleveland made the playoffs both years, but lost in the first round each time. The following year, the Cavs slumped to a 30–52 record and failed to make the playoffs. At season's end, Fitch announced he was stepping down after nine years as coach. A year later, the Cavs' owner, Nick Mileti, sold the team to Ted Stepien. Nobody knew much about Stepien, but the new owner soon proved that he didn't know much about basketball.

"Foots" Walker showed he also had quick hands by ranking sixth in the league in steals.

SELLING OUT THE CAV'S FUTURE

At first, Cleveland fans were excited about the club's new owner. They were encouraged to hear that Ted Stepien had both the money and the desire to buy high-priced stars if necessary. The Cavs definitely needed some help if they were to become a playoff contender again. But Stepien didn't spend his money wisely. He traded high draft choices for veteran players who were either near the end of their careers or just weren't that good. In Stepien's second season as owner, 1981–82, the Cavs lost 19 straight games. The team finished with a 15–67 record, exactly the same mark the first-year Cavs had posted 11 years before. And things would get worse before they got better.

The lowly Cavs didn't even have a first-round draft pick in

1982. The draft choice had been traded by Stepien to the Los Angeles Lakers for forward Don Ford. The Lakers used Cleveland's draft choice, the top pick overall, to take James Worthy, who would become an NBA All-Star and would help lead Los Angeles to four league titles. Later, the league told Stepien he could not trade any of Cleveland's future first-round draft picks.

After going through a series of coaches, Cleveland hired George Karl before the 1984–85 season. Karl built a team around high-scoring guard World B. Free, as well as forwards Roy Hinson and Phil Hubbard. Free was outspoken and cocky, but he had the talent to back up his boasts. "There's no one who can stop me, and I'm telling the truth," said Free, who changed his first name from "Lloyd" to "World" in the middle of his NBA career. "When I get hot, nobody can cool me down."

Free heated up enough in 1984–85 to lead the Cavaliers to the playoffs for the first time in seven years. But once again the team's winning ways ended in the first round of the playoffs, where the Cavs fell to Boston. The following year, Cleveland stumbled, posting a 29–53 record. Karl was fired after the season. To fill his position, the Cavs turned to a familiar face—Lenny Wilkens.

1 9 8 1
All-Star Mike Mitchell became the first Cav to score 2,000 points in a season.

AN OLD FRIEND RETURNS

After retiring as a player for the Cavs, Lenny Wilkens had coached at Portland and then joined the management of the Seattle SuperSonics. During the 1977–78 season, Wilkens replaced Seattle coach Bob Hopkins, leading the

The one and only World B. Free.

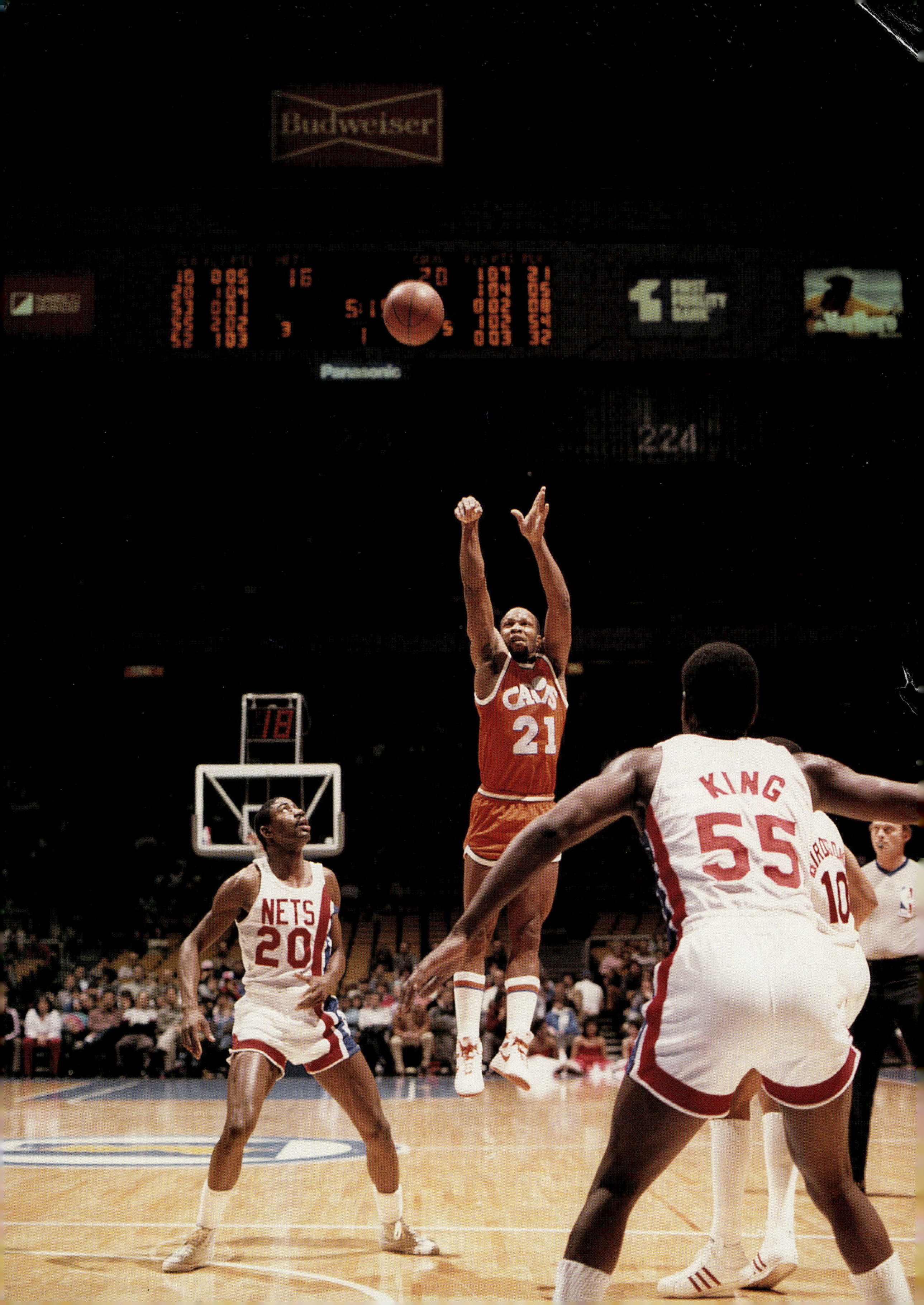

Budweiser
Panasonic
224
CAVS
21
KING
55
NETS
20
10

Roy Hinson, tough on the offensive boards.

Sonics to an NBA championship the following year. He coached the Sonics for several more years and then became the team's general manager. When the Cavs called about their coaching job, Wilkens did the same thing he had done as a player—he left Seattle for Cleveland.

As a coach, Wilkens believed in finding intelligent, team-oriented players and then giving them the freedom to work together to become a solid unit. He didn't believe in trying to guide a player's every move. Wilkens wanted players who felt comfortable playing their own game on the court.

When Lenny Wilkens first came to Cleveland as a player in 1972, he was asked to help turn a young team around. When he came to Cleveland as a coach, he was asked to rebuild a team with young players. The Cavs had the number one pick in the 1986 draft, as well as the number eight pick. Team management knew this draft was vital to the Cavs' future; Cleveland had to make the right choices. And the team did. In fact, few NBA teams have ever found so much talent in one draft.

The Cavs used the draft's top pick to take North Carolina center Brad Daugherty. They also selected guards Ron Harper from Miami of Ohio and Mark Price from Georgia Tech. Daugherty was a steady college performer who had played in the shadows of such great North Carolina stars as Michael Jordan and Sam Perkins.

But Daugherty was used to being overshadowed—even in his own family. One of his older brothers was a 7-footer weighing 290 pounds; the other was 6-foot-7 and 240 pounds. But the younger Daugherty soon became a match for his brothers, growing to be 6-foot-11 and weighing close

1 9 8 5

Phil Hubbard made 371 free throws to lead the Cavs his first year as a starter.

John "Hot Rod" Williams (pages 18–19).

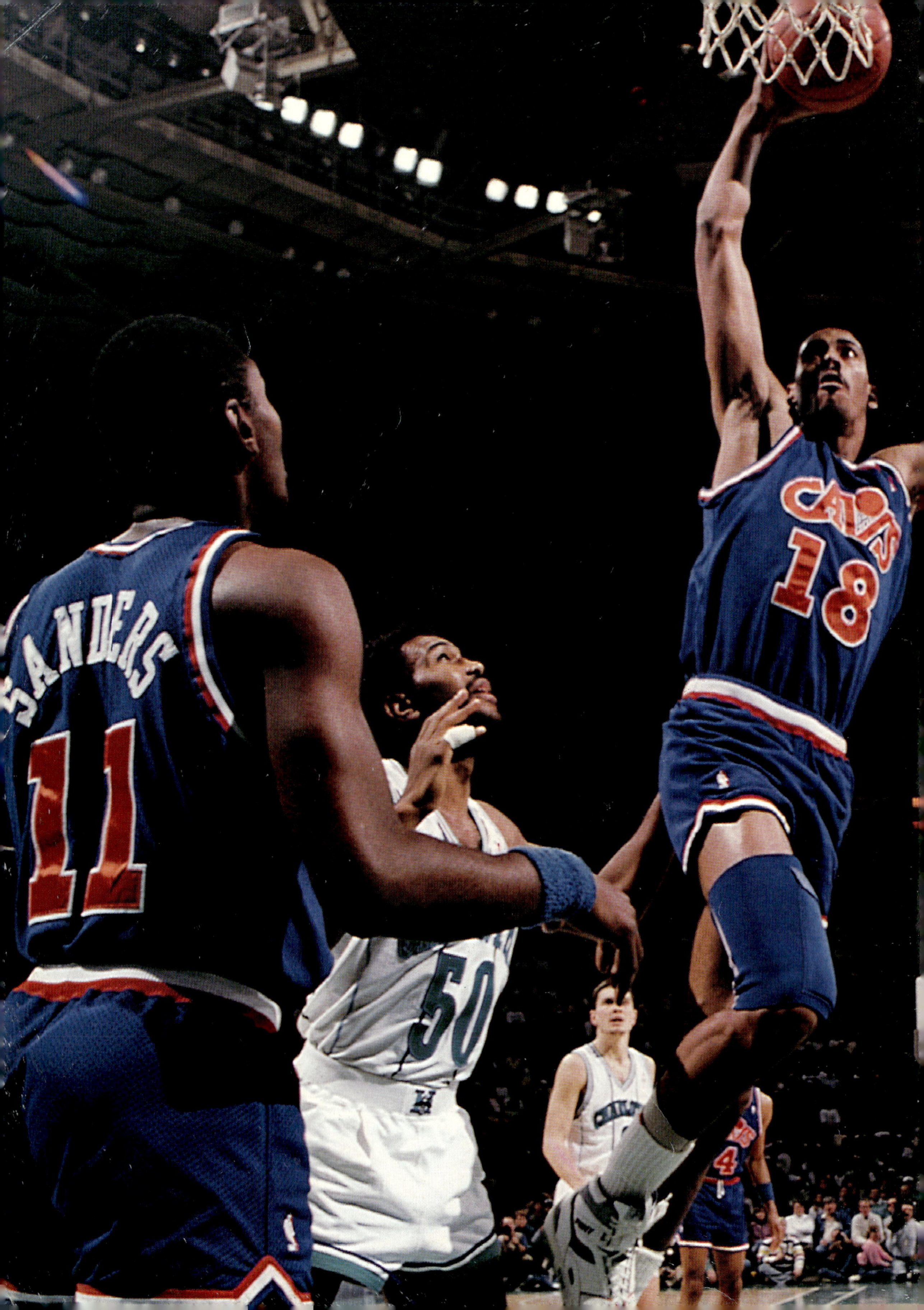
SANDERS
11
CAVS
18
50

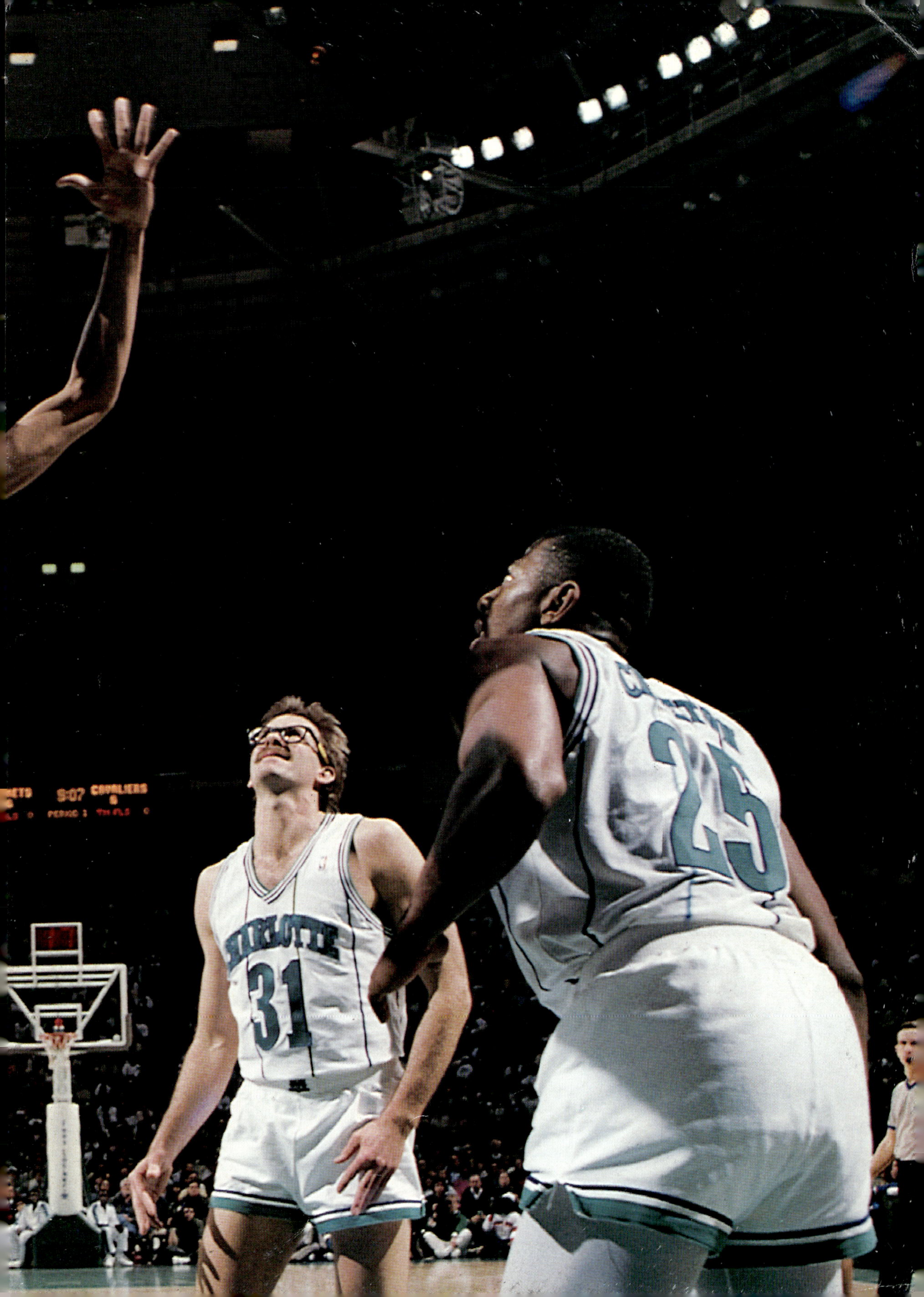
9:07 CAVALIERS
CHARLOTTE
31
25

John Bagley set a franchise record with 735 assists for the season.

to 250 pounds. When Daugherty enrolled at North Carolina, he was only 16 years old. By the time he was 17, he was a starter for the defending national champion Tar Heels; in fact, he started all four years he played at North Carolina. "We depend on Brad," said Tar Heels coach Dean Smith. "Mostly, we depend on his consistency."

Once Daugherty turned pro, he used his consistency and size to become one of the best young centers in the game. He also had a soft shooting touch and a knack for getting the big rebounds. During his early years with the Cavs, Daugherty developed into an effective shot-blocker, which

The talented Brad Daugherty.

made him one of the key components in Cleveland's defensive scheme. Daugherty wasn't spectacular, but he got the job done.

HARPER LEAPS TO NEW HEIGHTS

Daugherty may not have been flashy, but Ron Harper was. The Cavaliers took Harper, a little-known guard from Miami of Ohio, with the eighth pick in the 1986 draft. Harper never received much attention while he was in college, but the pro scouts knew how good he was. "He's capable of scoring 30 points a night," claimed Barry Hecker, Cleveland's director of scouting. "He's up with the best in the country. He reminds me of Julius Erving. He has that grace about him." Like Erving, Harper was a great leaper. He also had a nose for the basket. "I'm an Erving-type player," Harper stated. "When the game is on the line, I want the ball in my hands."

Harper was a natural talent, a player who made everything look easy on the basketball court. "He's so relaxed and graceful that he shows no signs of effort," Northern Illinois coach John McDougal said. "Put him anyplace on the court, and he can hurt you." Harper proved McDougal right in his rookie year in the NBA. His average of 22.9 points a game made him the highest-scoring Cavalier, as well as the highest scoring first-year player in the league. Many experts thought that Harper, not Indiana's Chuck Person, should have been named NBA Rookie of the Year during the 1986–87 season.

Harper and Daugherty led the Cavaliers to the playoffs in

Craig Ehlo made his first of 381 three-point shots as a Cavalier.

The high-scoring Ron Harper.

their second year in Cleveland, 1987–88. But the Cavs seemed cursed—they lost yet again in the first round, this time to the Chicago Bulls. Then, the following season, everything came together for the young team. In 1988–89, the Cavs finished with a franchise-record 57 victories, which was second only to the Detroit Pistons, the eventual NBA champion. Daugherty and Harper combined with forward Mike Sanders to give the team a strong offense and an intimidating defense. But the guy who really made the Cavs go was a point guard the team had almost given up on—Mark Price.

Brad Daugherty's 333 assists made him the best passing center in the league.

PRICE CASHES IN AT THE POINTS

Like Daugherty and Harper, Price was part of the Cavs' terrific college draft in 1986. But unlike them, he didn't have an instant impact on the team. In fact, the Cleveland management was so unimpressed with Price that the team selected another point guard, Kevin Johnson, in the first round of the 1987 draft. Everyone expected Johnson to come in and become the starting floor general. But Price made sure that didn't happen. He consistently outplayed Johnson both in practice and in games.

The Cavs soon traded Johnson and center Mark West to the Phoenix Suns for Larry Nance, who would prove to be a source of support for Price's talents. Price was now the player to run the Cleveland offense, which was a big load to place on the shoulders of a man barely six feet tall. But Price was a deadly shooter, even from the three-point range, and a great passer. "He's not the average point guard," said Detroit forward John Salley, a college teammate of Price's. "He

In a game vs. Atlanta, Mark Price made 19 of 20 free throws, a team record.

plays like he's 6-foot-5. He's a Larry Bird type. If a coach was to let him go, he'd have 40 points a night against anybody."

Price averaged 18.9 points and 8.4 assists per game for the Cavaliers during the 1988–89 season. He also made 90 percent of his free throws and was the third-best three-point shooter in the league. "I don't think I've ever had a point guard who fills the role as well as Mark does," said Lenny Wilkens, who had been a fan of Price's from the beginning. "I knew he was quicker than people were saying, and I could see he could shoot."

But Price's main job was to run the team and make sure that all of the other players got their shots. "We could easily design our offense so that one of us could score 25 or 30 points every night," explained Daugherty. "But with a young team and all the energy we have, that would be kind of foolish. This way we all become better players. Everyone has the opportunity to be the man. And it's up to each of us to take it."

While Price provided leadership, Nance came through with extra muscle inside. The 6-foot-10 forward's rebounding, solid defense, and overall excellent play was complemented by the abilities of Daugherty on the Cavs' front line. Despite their inside strength, the Cavs were unable to advance past the first round of the 1989 playoffs. Cleveland was once again eliminated by Michael Jordan and the Chicago Bulls. This time, however, it took a near miracle to end the Cavs' championship hopes so early.

The Cavs and Bulls split the first four games of the best-of-five series, with the final game scheduled in Cleveland's

Coliseum. That last game was close throughout, but the Cavs seemed assured of victory when guard Craig Ehlo, with just four seconds left, hit a clutch shot to put Cleveland ahead by a point. But it wasn't enough. Jordan then drove to the free-throw line, leaped, and launched a jump shot that hit nothing but net. The Bulls had won, and Cleveland's best season ever had come to an end.

TEAMWORK AND DEFENSE IN THE 1990s

The following year, 1989-90, injuries prevented the Cavaliers from performing at top form. Cleveland's injury problems continued during the 1990–91 season. A knee injury early in the year kept Mark Price out of the game for the remainder of the season—and the Cavs really missed him. The team had no one to control the offense—no one to make sure that everyone got their shots. The Cavs finished the year with a 33–49 record and failed to make the playoffs for the first time in four years.

The Cavs of the early 1990s played well, but they never got past the mighty Chicago Bulls in the playoffs. Frustrated by the consistent losses, Coach Wilkens resigned at the end of the 1991–92 season. He was replaced by Mike Fratello. As coach of the Atlanta Hawks through most of the 1980s, Fratello molded the team into one of the best and flashiest in the NBA—and one of the favorites of fans everywhere. But Fratello's first few seasons at Cleveland were plagued by injuries, and he didn't have the talented superstars he had coached in Atlanta to carry the team. Fratello responded by turning the Cavs into defensive specialists, which slowed

"Outsider" Steve Kerr sank more than 50 percent of his three-point shots to lead the league.

Terrell Brandon, the Cavs' leader on the court (pages 26–27).

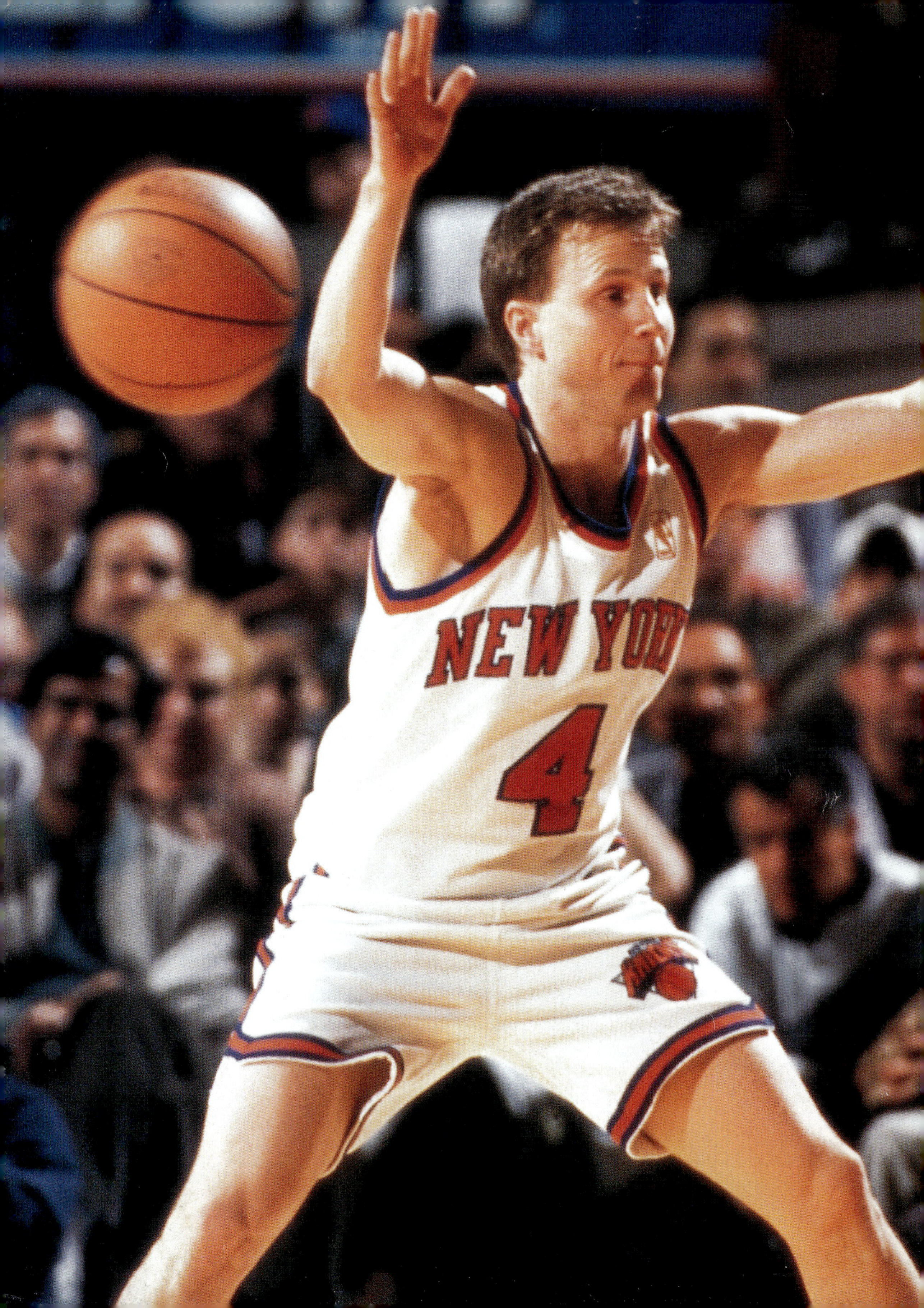
NEW YORK
4

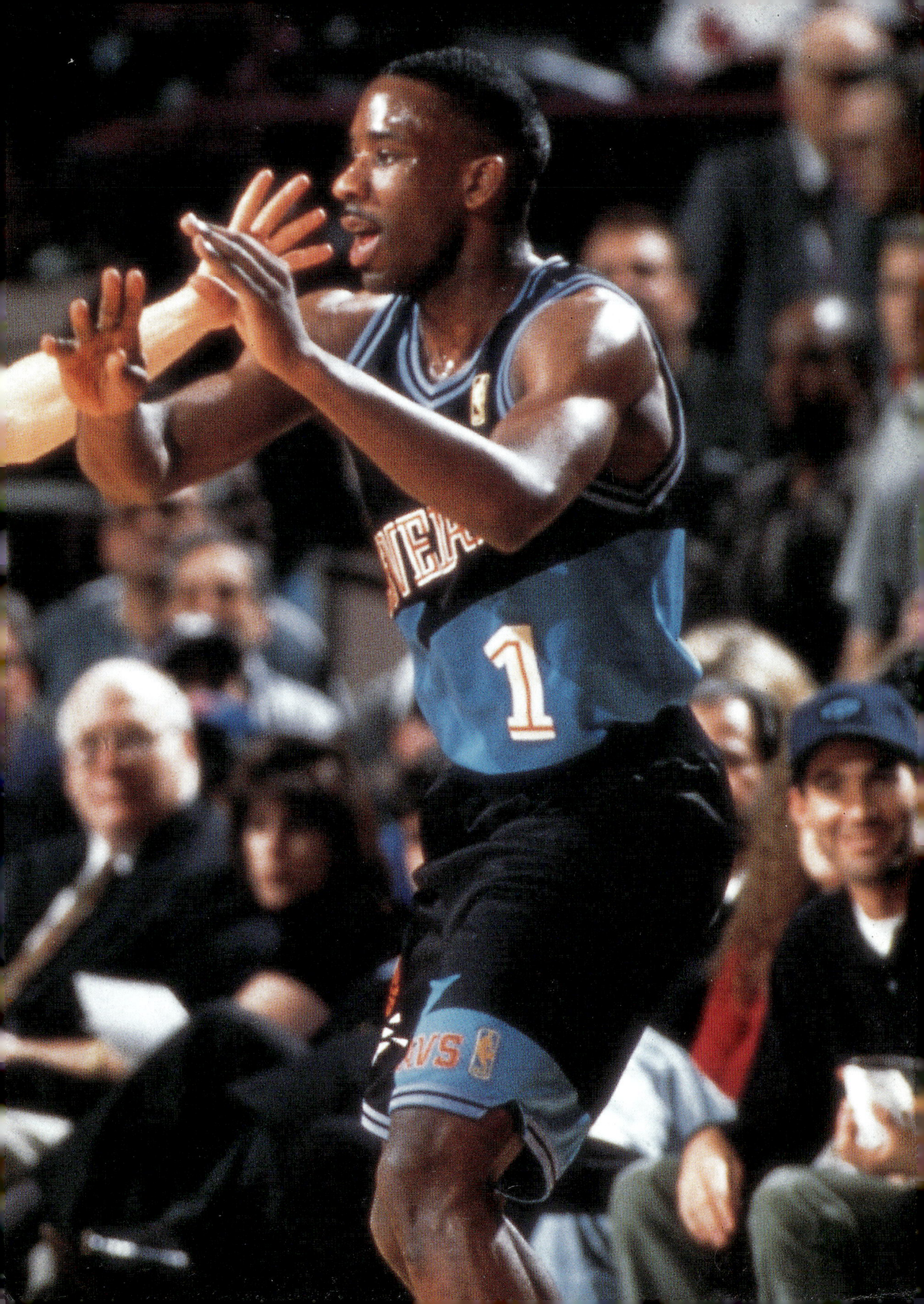

First-year All-Star Tyrone Hill led the Cavs with 765 total rebounds.

down the pace of Cleveland's games, even against high-scoring opponents.

Fratello replaced Daugherty, Nance, and Price with such younger players as Chris Mills, Bobby Phills, and team leader and starting point guard Terrell Brandon. Brandon was drafted out of Oregon in 1991, but it took the injury to Mark Price to give him a chance to play in Cleveland. Brandon proved he could lead the team, so the Cavaliers decided to trade Price, making Brandon the starting point guard.

The 1995–96 season was Brandon's breakthrough year. As the starting point guard, he played well enough to be selected as an All-Star. At 5-foot-11, Brandon was only the eighth player in NBA history under six feet tall to be selected as an All-Star. Though Brandon's reputation and stock rose around the NBA, he was the first to credit teamwork for Cleveland's success.

"We don't have any superstars on our team," Brandon said. "We just believe in working hard and going beyond expectations."

Coach Fratello echoed that sentiment, saying, "They try to find a way to win every night out. And it should be a statement that every club should be able to make about every team in the league. I'm not so sure that happens every night to be honest. This group does that. And that's one of the reasons why I have a very, very special feeling about the people we have here."

This sense of dedication led Fratello's Cavs to become defensive masters. In the 1995–96 season, Cleveland allowed an average of only 88.5 points per game—fewer than had ever been allowed in NBA history. Some critics thought that

Fratello's focus on defense wouldn't bring the team much success in the long run. But in the 1996–97 season the Cavs rose above their critics. Early on, they were allowing only 80.9 points per game. Their bench was outscoring their opponents' bench, and Cleveland was winning on the road. The Cavs were beating teams by an average of 8.8 points per game—second only to the Chicago Bulls. And Fratello had built his team with a lineup that featured none of the NBA's big stars.

Starting forward Chris Mills said the Cavs' success came from playing one game at a time. "Every day we take a look at the standings and see that we are up there and that is a good feeling. We know there can be streaks in the NBA where you can lose five or six games in a row or win five or six games in a row. We just have to take it one game at a time."

Mike Fratello's Cavs held opponents to an NBA-record 85.6 points per game.

The solid Bobby Phills.

Forward Chris Mills.

Bob Sura, Cleveland's dependable sixth man.

Top backup Bob Sura said, "Our defense and our unselfishness are what is best for us. That is how we win—by passing the ball and getting the other guys open shots instead of forcing one yourself."

The 1996–97 season produced some of the best all-around defensive play in NBA history, as other teams began copying the Cavs' recipe for excitement in the game. Like the city they play in, the Cavaliers are now the model of dedication and teamwork. They don't have any of the NBA's big-name stars, but Cleveland fans aren't worried about that—they know they can count on their favorite defensive specialists to start them on the road to a championship.

Locust Grove Elementary
31230 Constitution Hwy
Locust Grove, VA 22508

1806 5 2189302